He'd been seen! The truck pulled to a stop and Kevin Hoffman jumped out, afraid that the escaped convicts would chase him down. Instead they drove away, leaving him alone to die in the Devil's Desert.

Here, in a valley of sand, where the only green the eye can see for miles is the dark, dusty color of sage, everything looks alike. Rattlesnakes and lizards seek the shade of rocks at midday, but Kevin must keep moving, struggling to stay alive.

"Around here . . . without water . . . you might survive for twenty-four hours," his dad, a Marine officer, had said. Surely Dad would save him! Until then, Kevin had to keep his mind alert. But as time passed and the sun beat down, he began to feel himself losing control. . . .

LOST *in the* DEVIL'S DESERT

by Gloria Skurzynski
cover illustration by Richard Kriegler

This edition published in 1988, 1992 by
Willowisp Press, Inc., by arrangement
with Lothrop, Lee & Shepard Books.

Illustration copyright © 1992 by Willowisp Press.
Library of Congress Cataloging in Publication Data

Skurzynski, Gloria.
Lost in the Devil's Desert.

Summary: Eleven-year-old Kevin finds himself alone and lost in
the Utah desert, with only his wits to help him survive.

[1. Survival—Fiction.   2. Deserts—Fiction]
1. Title.

PZ7.S6287Lo   [Fic]   81-13667
ISBN: 0-87406-586-0

Printed in the United States of America.

10 9 8 7 6 5 4 3 2

One

I looked at my military watch to check the time. Ever since my dad had given it to me a week earlier, I'd checked the time about every five minutes. It was a great watch. The hours were numbered in digitals from 1 to 24, a whole day's worth.

The watch had one function I tried to ignore. It told the date. Even though I didn't look, I knew it was June 16. Five more days, and my dad would be gone.

Miles of sand dotted with sagebrush skimmed past the car window. The sight of all that desert twisted my insides, too, just the way the date on my watch did.

In five days we'd reach Nellis Air Force Base, in Nevada, where I'd say good-bye to my dad, maybe forever. He was being sent on a Joint Armed Forces mission to the Middle East. I didn't know what the mission was, because it was top secret, but Dad had just finished two months of intensive training in desert survival.

"What time is it, Kevin?" Dad asked from the front seat. He smiled at Mom, because he was kidding me—Dad had his own watch.

"Fourteen-fifteen," I answered. That means a quarter after two.

"We'll be in Spriggs pretty soon," Dad said. Spriggs, Utah, is where my great-grandmother lives. Since the town lies on the route to Nellis, we were planning to spend three days visiting Gram, as Dad calls her. Looking in the rearview mirror so that our eyes met, he said, "I think you're going to enjoy Spriggs, Kevin. You haven't seen it since you were too little to remember. The town is . . . 'anachronism' is the best word I can think of. That means something that belongs to a different time. Spriggs is pretty much the way it was sixty years ago, when your great-grandfather worked in the silver mine."

"Is it desert all around Spriggs," I asked, "like this stuff we're driving through?"

"Spriggs has trees and grass, and a few gardens from irrigation," he answered, "but yes, it's set in the middle of desert just like this."

I glanced again at the flat sand outside, then said, "Dad, you could stay alive in the Utah desert easier than in the Middle East, couldn't you? I mean, look, there are some plants growing out there."

"Around here . . . without water . . . mmmm, you might survive for twenty-four hours."

"No more desert talk, Bill. Please," Mom said to Dad. Dad and I had been talking a lot about desert survival during the three-day drive, and it was starting to get to Mom. She's a good military wife—I've heard Dad say that lots of times—but I guess enough was enough.

Dad's a career officer in the Marines, so he's been away a lot. I always missed him when he was gone, but before this I never worried about him too much. Maybe it's because I'm older now—almost twelve—but lately I've started to realize that my dad could get killed doing the job he does.

Dad was quiet until the car rounded a curve in the highway, then he announced, "Here it is, Kevin. Spriggs, Utah."

"This is Spriggs?" I asked. "Wow, what a dump!"

We'd started our drive to Spriggs from the Oregon coast. Dad was on leave, and he'd wanted a short vacation among some trees and ocean after all that training in the Mojave Desert. The difference between that beautiful ocean scenery and Spriggs was . . . well, like the difference between a fancy aquarium and a chicken coop.

On the main street of Spriggs, almost every other house was leaning sideways, ready to fall over. Some of them *had* fallen over—the narrow lots were full of bricks, boards, and broken glass.

"Why does Gram stay here?" I asked.

"It's home to her," Dad told me. "Gram has lived in Spriggs since she was a bride. It wasn't so shabby then; it was a busy mining town until the silver ran out."

We turned on a short side street and parked in front of the funny old house where my great-grandmother lives. The porch sagged in the middle like a cantaloupe rind. A huge spruce tree filled the small front yard, looking strong and healthy next to the droopy wooden house.

We climbed the rickety steps, and Mom was about to knock on the screen door, but she looked through the screen and smiled. "Gram's asleep in her chair," she whispered. "Let's go in quietly. We don't want to startle her."

Inside, the house smelled old—musty with a whiff of sour. The living room was so small that when I'd taken three steps, I was right in front of the chair where my great-grandma dozed.

She was tiny, and *old*. Her face had as many lines as a fancy spiderweb. Her eyelids fluttered, then she looked straight at me and said, "Bill, you're here."

"I'm not Bill," I told her. "I'm Kevin."

I didn't know old ladies could blush, but Gram did. Blushed and smiled, and in the smile her false teeth looked too big for her face. "Of course you're Kevin," Gram said. "I don't know what I could have been thinking of."

After she'd hugged me, then Mom and Dad, Gram sat us down to what she called "a late lunch or an early supper, whichever you want to name it." She hurried around, bringing us plates of ham, sliced tomatoes, deviled eggs, and something she called "pickle lily." Then she hovered behind our chairs to make sure that our plates were full.

"That was great, Gram," Dad said, after all of us had eaten as much as we could hold. "Just like I remembered. Now, if you ladies don't mind, I think we menfolk will leave you for a while. I want to take Kevin to meet Barney."

"That old reprobate!" Gram snorted. "He's a boozer and a cusser."

Mom and Dad both laughed. "Heavens!"

9

Mom said. "This Barney sounds like he'll be a bad influence on Kevin."

"Since we're only going to be here for three days," Dad answered, "Kevin can take his chances."

Gram was still tsk-tsking as Dad and I walked down the porch steps, hearing the screen door squeak shut behind us.

Two

WALKING along the streets—or street, I should say, because there was only one main street—I noticed that Spriggs looked even more tumbledown than it had from the car. There was no sidewalk, only worn, cracked asphalt that sagged in the middle. Everything in Spriggs sagged in the middle.

"That's Barney's place," Dad said, pointing to a sign that said "Barney's Garage."

"A garage? You mean people in Spriggs have cars?" I joked.

"Ha, ha, very funny," Dad answered. "But listen, comedian, Barney's an old friend of mine, so show a little respect when you meet him."

"Yes, *sir*!" I said, snapping a sharp military salute. Dad aimed a pretend clout at my arm, but he was grinning.

We walked past two antique gas pumps and

pushed open the door to the garage's office, if you could call it that. And there was Barney. Older than the gas pumps, wearing a gray work shirt, pants that looked like they'd been made out of a Marine blanket, and suspenders two inches wide. He'd been tilted backward on a wooden chair, but when he saw us, the chair legs hit the floor with a bang.

"Bill!" Barney shouted, his wide face creased in a huge smile. "Well, I'll be a son of a gun. Bill Hoffman! You're a sight to turn a mangy coyote into a sheepdog."

"How are you, Barney?" Dad asked, pumping the old man's hand.

"Can't complain, Bill. This must be your kid, huh? Looks just like you did when you was a tad—that mop of dark hair that won't stay down. Remember how you used to flatten yours with Brylcreem? What's the boy's name?"

"Kevin," I said, stepping forward to shake hands.

"How old are you, boy?"

"Eleven."

"Kevin Eleven, huh? Eleven Kevin." Barney laughed hard and slapped his thick thigh. Even though his wisecrack wasn't very funny, I knew I should laugh with Barney, but I couldn't bring it off. I mean, I can joke with my mom and dad, but around new people I sort of freeze.

"I'll be twelve in three more weeks," I told him, sounding too serious.

"Twelve's close to bein' a man," Barney said, "but still boy enough for funnin'. Does Kevin like junk piles the way you used to?" he asked my dad.

Dad's eyes warmed like he was remembering something special. "Still got the old pile of junk in back, Barney?"

"You bet. Since there ain't no money in town these days, folks fixes up anything that breaks down. My junk pile's got parts and pieces of stuff that you couldn't find anywhere else in the whole U.S. of A."

Dad nudged me. "Go on around back, Kevin, and introduce yourself to Barney's junk heap. It's like an archaeological dig. The stuff on top is the newest. The farther down you go, the older the junk gets."

"Yeah," Barney agreed. "If anyone ever got to the bottom, they'd probably find a Ute Indian tomahawk."

I couldn't imagine why my dad wanted me to look at a junk pile, but I walked around to the back of the garage. When I got there, the heap did look interesting, I had to admit. All kinds of stuff was piled as high as my shoulders. On the top I found a headlight, a steering wheel, and a battered bike with no tires.

The bike might have possibilities, I thought. Since worn automobile tires were scattered all over the lot, Barney might have some bike tires, too. I yanked down the bike and checked it over. The chain drooped, but when I pushed the pedals, the rear wheel spun. Maybe if I fixed the bike, Dad and I could ride it for the couple of days we'd be in Spriggs.

"Come on, Kevin," I heard Dad call after a while. "We'd better get back to Gram's. She probably wants to feed us again. You can come to Barney's tomorrow if you want to."

* * * * *

The next day was DD Day Minus Four. That was the code I'd made up for my own private use—Dad's Departure Day minus whatever time was left before he had to go.

Gram fixed us a breakfast of pancakes and honey, strawberries and cream. And I drank two big glasses of milk. I remember every bite of that breakfast. It was the last meal I had for a long time.

After I'd stuffed myself, I pushed back the chair and said, "I think I'll go over to

Barney's."

"That old reprobate," Gram sniffed. "He's a boozer and a cusser."

I guess I looked surprised—those were the exact words she'd used the day before. Dad leaned over to whisper, "Gram's been calling Barney the same names for years. In spite of what she says, she really likes Barney."

"Did you find anything usable in the junk pile?" Mom asked me.

"Yeah. An old bike I think I can fix," I said on my way to the door.

"Wait a minute, Kevin," Mom called. "It's chore time. Dad is going to see about fixing the front steps. Gram and I will make the beds. You do the dishes."

Boy! By my watch, I wasted exactly forty-nine minutes doing those dumb dishes. I wanted to hurry up and fix that old bike so Dad and I could ride around Spriggs. He'd pedal, and I'd sit on the handlebars the way we used to when I was little.

On the way to Barney's, I noticed a kid about my age walking along the asphalt toward me. When we got close, I turned my eyes away, because I didn't know if guys in Spriggs said hi to strangers. We passed each other without speaking.

What would it be like to be a kid living in a

place like Spriggs? I wondered. Gram had said that only about a hundred people were left in town, almost all of them old folks. There were always bunches of kids around me, in all the different schools I'd gone to, but I bet I'd felt more alone than that boy in Spriggs ever did.

When I got to Barney's, he said, "Well, if it ain't Kevin Eleven. How you doin', tad?"

"Okay. Barney, there's a bike on your junk pile. I saw it yesterday."

"Oh, yeah. I found that about a month ago when I was drivin' around in the desert. Found it in a dry wash. Don't know how it ever got out there."

"What's a dry wash?" I asked.

"Well, when it rains in the desert, which it don't very often, there ain't no trees or grass to soak up the water. So the runoff cuts channels in the sand, like stream beds. After the water's gone, the channels are called dry washes."

"That's interesting," I said, trying to sound polite. "Do you have any tires that would fit that bike? I can pay for them. I have a couple of dollars."

"Tires and tubes, boy. Those old-fashioned bikes need inner tubes. I might could find some for you, if you give me a minute. But Bill Hoffman's son don't need to pay for anything around here."

I didn't know how to thank him without sounding dumb, so I didn't say anything. When I brought the bike around front, Barney was pulling inner tubes out of a cupboard in the garage. "Tires in here, too," he said. "We'll need a couple of wrenches, to put them on with. See that pickup truck over there? Climb up in the back and bring whatever wrenches you can find."

A beat-up Chevy pickup truck sat parked in a corner of the lot. Wooden slats had been built up on the sides of the truck bed about three feet higher than the metal sides, so Barney could haul tall loads, I supposed. I climbed over the tailgate and landed on a big pile of tools. Where would the wrenches be in that mess? I wondered. I didn't want to start throwing tools around, so I sat there for a few minutes while my eyes adjusted to the shade of the truck.

Then I heard voices, speaking low. When I looked out through the spaces between the wooden slats, I saw two men standing about six feet away. Their heads were close together and they were talking like they didn't want anyone to hear what they were saying. They stared at the garage, and then one of them stopped talking while he lit a cigarette.

The man holding the cigarette was blond. His face was red from sunburn, and full of acne scars. The other man was short and dark, with a lot of straight black hair. After a minute I realized that he was an Indian. Both of them were dressed the same, in faded Levis and white T-shirts with "Mountain State Penitentiary" lettered on them. That made me smile, because I like T-shirts that say funny things. I was wearing one that said "Front" and "Back," but "Back" was on the front and "Front" was on the back.

The blond guy flipped his cigarette away, walked to the cab of the truck, and looked in the window. He pointed to the dashboard and said just one word to the Indian: "Keys."

Three

I thought maybe something funny was going on, so I stayed very quiet in the back of the truck. The wooden sides hid me from the two men, but I could watch them through the spaces between the slats.

They walked over to the garage and went inside where Barney was rummaging for the bike tires.

"Can you give me some change for the pay phone?" the blond one asked. His voice came out clearly from the open door.

"I don't have a pay phone here," Barney answered, "but you can use my phone and pay me for the call."

"Well, give me some change anyway, okay?" the man said. I could see him through the garage window. He put his hand into his pocket and took out a wrinkled bill.

Barney went to the cash register and

punched open the cash drawer. While he was counting out the change the Indian circled behind him, picked up a gasoline can, and before I even had a chance to yell, hit Barney over the head with the can. As Barney sagged against the cash register, the Indian hit him again. Barney fell to the floor, and I felt my stomach go sick. Right then I realized that those T-shirts were no joke. Those guys were escaped convicts.

The blond guy grabbed money from the cash drawer, and the two of them ran right toward me and jumped into the cab of the truck. I sat in the back, too shocked to do anything. As the engine caught and the truck lurched, I dived down to the floor of the truck bed and hoped the two men hadn't seen me.

I had to get out of there, but how? The truck was picking up speed. If it stopped for a red light or a stop sign, I could jump over the tailgate, but I didn't think Spriggs had any red lights or stop signs. Then it was too late. We turned onto the highway and started going really fast.

Even at that speed, I thought about jumping out of the moving truck, but it was bouncing around so much that I wouldn't have been able to balance myself to jump safely. Anyway, if I stood up the two thieves could see me through the window in the back of the truck cab. I wiggled around to face the window so I could watch them. That way I'd know if they turned around and saw me, and if they did, I'd jump, no matter how fast the truck was going.

The Indian was talking excitedly to the other guy, who was driving. He was turned around in his seat so far that if he'd turned his head just a few inches farther, he'd have seen me. I noticed a piece of canvas folded in the corner of the truck bed. As soon as the Indian turned forward in his seat, I pulled the canvas over me. It was big enough to cover me completely, even my head, but I pushed it back a little so I could watch what was going on in front.

It was murder riding in the back of that truck. Not only was I bouncing hard on the floor, but the loose tools were banging against me. The luminous face of my watch showed 10:53. As the truck sped on, I kept track of the time, figuring that we were traveling about a mile a minute. After thirty-six minutes—thirty-six miles of getting beat up by the tools—I felt the truck make a sharp left turn off the highway.

Maybe they were going to stop, I hoped. If they did, I'd jump out and run like the devil. The thought of it gave me cold chills, because

I didn't know whether they had a gun.

But they didn't stop. The truck kept going, on a little side road, it felt like, because the bouncing got a whole lot worse. I tried to work backward so that I could brace my Nike shoes against the tailgate, but the motion of the truck just bounced me forward again. Then the side road must have ended—the truck went slower, and lurched from side to side as though we were hitting some big dips in the dirt.

The minutes just dragged by. My watch showed 12:20 and we were still moving, but so much slower that I couldn't guess the distance we'd traveled. It started to get really hot under that canvas—after the truck had slowed there wasn't much air blowing around me, and the sun must have been blazing. I moved the canvas off my head a little more to get some air. Just at that minute the Indian looked back through the cab window and saw me.

His eyes opened wide and he stared for a few seconds like he couldn't believe what he was seeing. Then he yelled something to the other man. The truck stopped with a jolt.

I leaped over the tailgate and started to run the minute my feet hit the ground. I half expected to hear gunshots and to feel bullets zapping around me, so I ran zigzag, like a football player. The ground I was running on was rocky and sandy. I slipped a few times and almost fell, but I kept running until my chest felt like it would split. Then I saw a big boulder, and I dived behind it.

There was no sound except the pounding of my heart and the gasping of my breath. After about a minute I snaked along the ground so I could see around the edge of the boulder.

The truck looked far away. The two men were standing beside the truck, looking toward me. They must have known that I was behind the boulder, but they just stood there, watching. They didn't even make a move to come after me.

I couldn't believe what happened next: They got into the truck and drove away. I thought maybe they were going to circle around and drive toward me, but they drove away. Moving clear of the boulder, I watched the truck grow smaller and smaller in the distance, until it went over the top of a hill and disappeared from sight.

Four

A S soon as I got over feeling relieved that I wasn't shot full of holes, I looked around. I was on sand, in a big, wide valley of sand dotted with low bushes of sagebrush. On all sides of me were mountains. The sage seemed to march about halfway up the mountains, but the mountain tops were bare gray rock. One of the mountains wasn't gray, though. It was closer and a lot lower than the rest, and had a reddish color to it.

By that time I'd pretty much stopped being scared, and I started to get mad. Only four days left before my dad went away, and it looked like I'd waste one of them just getting back to Spriggs. By the time I walked the road back to the highway and called my dad to come get me, it would be close to dinnertime.

From where I was standing, I couldn't see the road at all. Scanning the sand, I walked in the direction I thought the road had been, but it wasn't until I came across the tire tracks that I was sure I'd found it.

It didn't look like a road. It was just a pathway about six feet wide, a little lower than the sand on either side of it, with hardly any sage growing in it. I stared down at the tire tracks, wondering what kind of road that was. It curved away from me on both sides until it was lost in rows of sagebrush, looking more like a dry river bed than a road. What was it Barney had said? A dry wash!

So we'd been driving along a dry wash. But I knew we must have driven off a road somewhere, so all I had to do was follow the dry wash back to where the road began. I turned and started to retrace the tire tracks.

After a few feet I stopped. Maybe it would be better to take a look at the whole area. Maybe if I got on higher ground, I could see a house or some sign of civilization nearby, where I could go to call my dad. That way, I wouldn't have to walk all the way back to the highway.

The red mountain was closer than the rest of the mountains; in fact, it didn't look far away at all. And it looked like it would be easy to climb, so I could get high enough to have a good view.

I'd gone just a little way toward the mountain when something exploded from the sage in front of me. My heart jumped, but it was only a jackrabbit. He bounced and leaped through the sagebrush, his long ears sticking up over the dusty green leaves. If there are jackrabbits here, I thought, there must be water. Maybe I'll be able to see it when I get up on the mountain.

The red mountain was taking longer to reach than I expected, and the sun was boiling me. I sat down to take off my Nikes and my crew socks. Tying the toes of the socks together, I wrapped them around my neck like a scarf to keep the sun from burning my neck.

I tried walking in my bare feet, but too many little rocks in the sand hurt my toes, and worse, the sand was so hot it scorched the bottoms of my feet. So I put my Nikes back on, over my bare feet.

As I walked I kicked up sand, which slid down inside my shoes. Pretty soon I felt like I was walking on sandpaper. I thought I'd better put my socks back on, or else my feet would be rubbed raw by the sand in my shoes. When I did, my neck started to burn again.

Right then I made a pretty good guess why cowboys dress the way they do. High boots must keep sand from getting down to their feet. Neckerchiefs protect their necks from sunburn, and Western hats keep the blazing sun out of their eyes. I wished I had one right then—a nice, big cowboy hat.

When I finally got to the bottom of the red mountain, it looked higher than it had from a distance, but it still wasn't big for a mountain. "Mountain" wasn't even the right name for it.

At my California school, which had let out just ten days before, we'd studied earth science. The teacher liked me because I always did my homework, and she gave me an A. So I should have been able to remember the different names for land elevations.

Butte, or mesa—no, the red elevation wasn't either of those. Ridge . . . knoll? Yeah, that was it. Low elevations are called knolls.

I walked up a gully in the side of the knoll until it got too steep, then I climbed from one boulder to another till I was high enough to see everything below.

The whole sandy valley was spread out in front of me, completely surrounded by a circle of middle-sized mountains (ridges? I think so.) Behind the ridges were high mountain peaks, row after row until the last ones in the distance disappeared in a blue haze. The mountains were all different shapes. Some of them had tops like upside-down ice cream cones;

others were round and flattened as though a big hand had squashed them. The peaks of the high mountains in the distance looked like the chipped edges of Indian arrowheads—they seemed to rise up out of each other like ocean waves.

I studied the floor of the valley. It looked green, but I knew that the green was only sagebrush. There wasn't a single tree as far as I could see, and I could see pretty far. No roads, no houses, no cars, no smoke from fires, not a sign of life, nothing. Just total emptiness.

Five

A S I sat there scowling at that great big view of emptiness, I noticed that my back no longer felt hot. The sun had passed behind the red knoll, casting shade on my back. I flattened myself against the rock so that the shade covered all of my body. It felt a whole lot cooler.

I'm going to need water pretty soon, I told myself. Once again my eyes swept the valley, more carefully this time. If there was any water, in a spring or even a little water hole, there ought to be some green plants growing around it. Not the dark, dusty green of the sagebrush, but bright, fresh green. I scanned the whole floor of the valley, but I couldn't see any bright green at all.

Okay, I thought, no water. The next best thing for me is to go back to the dry wash and follow the tire tracks to the highway. I looked at my watch: 15:28, almost 3:30. I cussed out loud because of all the time I was wasting, but I knew it would be smart to wait in the shade until the sun got lower and less hot. Then I could make up the time by walking faster.

The inside of my mouth felt dry. One of my dad's survival tricks came to my mind: Put a pebble in your mouth and suck on it. It worked. A trickle of spit wet my tongue.

When I climbed down from the red knoll, the shadows were getting longer. I noticed little round balls of stuff lying on the ground, so I knelt down to examine them. They looked like animal droppings, from small animals, I guessed, because they were about as big as marbles. They must have been from jackrabbits.

But the little balls of manure were all over the place, and if jackrabbits had left that much stuff behind, there ought to be hundreds of jackrabbits hopping around in the bushes. I'd only seen one. I couldn't figure it out.

I did see lizards skittering around, though. About every couple of minutes one would scoot away from me across the sand. The lizards were little fellows, about five inches long, and half of that was tail. They were kind of cute.

One of the lizards was sunning himself on a

big rock, and he stayed real still even when I came up right next to him. I guess he thought he blended in with the rock so I couldn't see him. I whipped out my hand to catch him, but he was too fast for me. All I got was his tail, and I mean I *really* got his tail! The lizard was gone, but his tail was flip-flopping in my fingers! After I got over the shock, I felt kind of bad—that poor lizard needed his tail a whole lot more than I did. When I dropped it on the sand, it looked like a little worm.

It was time to quit fooling around if I was going to make it back to Gram's by dinnertime. I followed my own footprints in the sand back to the dry wash, then checked my direction. I remembered where I was when the truck disappeared, and I was pretty sure which way to turn to go back the way the truck had come. I started to walk, still sucking on the pebble. The sand kept sinking under my feet.

My arms and face felt hot, and they were turning red. Then a breeze started to blow. The air was still hot, and with the breeze stirring it up it felt like hot air coming from a furnace vent. The breeze blew hard, blowing sand in my eyes. Maybe it's going to rain, I thought.

It didn't rain. It just blew. Harder and harder. My skin started to feel tight from the hot air blowing on it, as though someone was pulling both sides of my face. My eyes stung from the sand in them. I sat down and pulled off my T-shirt to wipe my eyes. Grains of sand peppered my bare back. After a while I put on my shirt and started to walk again, but it was harder to see the tire tracks because the wind was blowing them away. It doesn't matter, I told myself. I can just follow the dry wash.

The wind blew for two whole hours, turning cooler and cooler as the sun went down behind the peak of a mountain. All that time I kept plowing through sand. Walking in loose sand is something like walking through deep snow— your steps never feel solid. I was getting nervous; daylight wasn't going to last much longer, and I needed to find the road because I had to get back to my dad. It was already later than dinnertime.

My stomach kept gurgling. I didn't need its growling to remind me that I was starved. My watch said 20 hours, or 8:00 P.M.—almost 11 hours had gone by since my last meal. Mom and Dad and Gram must have given up waiting for me by then. They were probably sitting down to dinner, or supper, as Gram called it.

The night before, Gram had fixed us fried steaks for a late supper. That was the first time I'd ever eaten steak that was fried. My mother always broiled our steaks, or else Dad

34

cooked them outside on the charcoal grill.

After Gram took the steaks out of the frying pan, she'd sliced cooked potatoes into the hot grease. Gram called them "fries," which surprised me. The kind of fries I was used to came from McDonald's, and looked a whole lot different than Gram's.

All that thinking about food would have made my mouth water, except I didn't have any spit left to water my mouth with. Then I forgot about food, because the dry wash disappeared.

It just disappeared! I ran back and forth looking for tire tracks, but of course there weren't any because they'd all been blown away. Just about then the wind stopped, but the lack of wind didn't do me any good because the tire tracks had already been wiped out.

I panicked! My hands started to shake and my breath came in short, jerky puffs. "I'm lost!" I yelled, and then I started to yell a lot of other things, like "Help!" and "Daddy, come and get me." But that was crazy, because there was nobody to hear me, and my dad didn't have any idea where I was or what had happened. They must have found Barney by then, but what could Barney tell them except that his truck was gone?

I hollered until my throat hurt, my yells bouncing around in the eerie quiet of the desert. Twilight filled the valley with frightening shadows. I felt totally alone, like I was the last person left in a dark, empty world, lost in an immense vacuum that could suck me under until I disappeared.

Crouching on the ground, I covered my head with my arms to hide from the silence. I was scared out of my skull, because I didn't have any idea what I should do. I was a whole lot more scared than the only other time I'd been lost, when I was eight years old. That was altogether different, because I wasn't alone that time. I was with Jeffrey, after the movie. I would have given anything to have Jeffrey with me right then, in the desert.

I've always had trouble making friends. I guess it's because we move so much. I've been in a different school almost every year since I started kindergarten. But that year, the year I was eight, I had a friend for a while. Jeffrey. He was in my class at school in Norfolk, Virginia.

One Saturday afternoon Jeffrey's father drove us to the movies. "Wait outside after the show's over," he told us, "and I'll come back to pick you up." We bought our tickets and went inside, two little kids excited about going to a show alone, without any grown-ups.

It was a horror film, with a monster that looked like a combination of dinosaur and sea slug. The monster ate a lot of people, and drowned some. Halfway through the movie, Jeffrey got so scared he ran out of the theater. There was nothing I could do except follow him.

It would have been more than an hour before Jeffrey's father came to pick us up, but Jeff didn't want to wait. "I know the way home, so we'll walk," he said.

I'd only lived in Norfolk for a couple of months, and I didn't know my way around at all, but I believed Jeffrey when he said he could get us home. We walked and walked, out of the downtown area where the theater was, into neighborhoods where there were houses and yards and kids riding bikes. "I know where I'm going," Jeff said every time I questioned him. "Just shut up and come on."

We must have walked about thirty blocks when I started to cry, because I knew we were lost. "I don't care what you do," I told Jeff, "but I'm going to ask someone if we can use their phone. I'm going to call my mom."

Jeff looked worried. He waited on the curb while I knocked on someone's door. The lady let me come inside to use the phone. She was real nice to me, even gave me some cookies.

"Where in the world are you?" Mom asked when I called her. "Jeff's dad went to pick up you boys a long time ago, but he couldn't find you anywhere." I gave her the address that the lady told me, and Mom said she'd tell Jeff's father.

When Jeff's dad drove up, he jumped out of the car, grabbed Jeff, and gave him a couple of hard whacks on the butt. All the way home he kept yelling at Jeff about what a stupid, disgusting kid he was, although he didn't say a single word to me.

After that Jeffrey wouldn't be my friend any more. Maybe he was mad because he got smacked and yelled at and I didn't. Or maybe he was afraid I'd tell the kids at school that Jeff turned chicken and ran out of the theater. But I never told anyone.

Being lost in the desert in the evening was a whole lot worse than being lost with Jeffrey in broad daylight. When the moon came up, it was just a little sliver that didn't give any light. A thumbnail moon, my mom called it. Since I couldn't see well enough to walk, and since I didn't know which way to walk anyway, I tried to calm down so I could think what to do.

It didn't take me long to figure out that there were no choices. I'd have to spend the night where I was. As soon as it got light in the morning, I'd start out. That way I'd make it back to Gram's by breakfast. At least by breakfast, I kept telling myself.

Lying on the sand, I tried to swallow to ease the dryness in my throat. It was dry as much from fright as from thirst. The sand wasn't very soft. I couldn't get my body into a comfortable position. Every time I rolled over, I landed on a rock.

Rocks. What was it about rocks? There was something about rocks and water. Piles of rocks. Something Dad learned about ancient people who lived in the desert near the Holy Lands.

That was it! I jumped up. Those ancient people piled up rocks because dew collected on them in the night. They used the dew from the rock piles to water their plants.

Scrambling around in the dusk feeling for rocks, I managed to collect a pile about two feet high. Please, I prayed, let there be dew on these rocks in the morning.

Six

THE sand still had some warmth in it from the heat of the day, and the warmth felt good on the sore muscles of my legs. Lying on my back, I saw that over the western edge of the mountains the sky still had a faint tinge of color where the sun had gone down. A few stars were lighting up over my head.

The sky grew darker so slowly that I couldn't really notice it; I could just sort of feel it happening. More stars came out, first a handful at a time, then whole clusters of constellations. It was the first time I'd ever been out at night in a place where there was no ground light at all—no glow from streetlights, not even lamplight from a single house. After a while I almost forgot to be scared, because I was so fascinated by the sky.

The stars seemed to be in layers: the brilliant ones close enough to touch; the ones that were just bright, farther away; and the dimmest ones so buried in space that I had to concentrate to see them. When the sky reached its darkest, the stars got their brightest. The Milky Way kept thickening, making a huge wide path that spanned the sky from one edge to the other, almost solid white, so bright I could hardly find any pinpoints of blackness in the whole ceiling of the galaxy.

It was the most fantastic thing I ever saw. If only my mom and dad could have been there to share it with me.

Mom and Dad. What were they doing then? How did my mother feel when I turned up missing? She would have waited for me to come back to Gram's, and when I didn't, maybe she walked over to Barney's to look for me. Maybe *she* was the one who found Barney unconscious, and then she would have searched all over for me until she realized I was gone.

Poor Mom. She was already upset about Dad leaving, and now this! My throat got all tight, feeling sorry for her, and for myself, too. She always tried so hard to make it up to me when Dad was away. She played games with me—Battleship, and Mastermind, and three-dimensional tic-tac-toe. I've been told I have a logical mind; I'm good at that kind of game, and at math and jigsaw puzzles. So usually I beat Mom, but she seemed to like it when I won.

More than anything in the world I wanted to be in my own bed with my mom coming in to say goodnight, bending over to hug me like she'd done the night before, at Gram's. I'd pretended to be asleep—big guys like me aren't supposed to like hugs. Would it have hurt me to put my arms around her for a change? I wished I had another chance.

But I wasn't in my warm bed, I was shivering God-only-knew where. All the heat had gone out of the sand. It's hard to believe how a desert can change from hot to cold after the sun goes down. It was a terrible night; I couldn't sleep for very long at a time. I kept waking up, partly because I was cold, but mostly because I was so thirsty. My throat hurt worse than it did the time I had strep throat, and my tongue got so swollen it filled my whole mouth. Each time I woke up I looked at the luminous face of my watch. After midnight my mind kept repeating "DD Day Minus Three." Three days left.

Even though I was curled up on the sand hugging my knees, I couldn't get warm. I tried to bury myself in the sand for warmth, but the sand was too full of rocks for me to dig it up with my bare hands. All I got was a handful of broken fingernails.

After a night that seemed like it would never end, the sky began to turn pale behind one of the mountains. Pretty soon I was able to see some of the sagebrush around me, so I gave up trying to sleep and got onto my feet. My head ached so much that it made me dizzy, but I forced myself to stand till the dizziness passed. My leg muscles were full of cramps. After I rubbed them for a while, they didn't hurt as much and I was able to move.

The first thing I did was check the rocks I'd piled the night before. The rocks on top of the pile felt dry on the surface, but when I moved them I could feel a little bit of dampness on the rocks in the center of the pile. Very carefully, I lifted the damp rocks and licked them. By the time I got to the bottom of the pile, my throat seemed to be working better, and I could swallow.

Pink streaks colored the sky where the sun was going to rise. That was east. I needed to settle on one direction, so I wouldn't walk in circles.

One of my geography teachers used to say, "Stand with your arms stretched straight out from your sides. Point to the east with your right hand. Your left hand will point to the west. Your nose will point to the north." So I followed my nose and headed north, because that was the direction I'd been traveling before the dry wash ended.

Although the sky was turning a pale blue, the air was still cold. It would be full daylight before the sun finally made it over the peak of a high mountain in the distance, and that was good, because as long as the sun stayed hidden behind the mountain, the desert would be cool enough for me to walk without getting dehydrated by the sun's rays. That is, if the wind didn't start to blow again. Dad said that wind could dry out a person almost as fast as the hot sun could.

I had to force myself to keep moving because I felt so rotten. Soon after the sun cleared the top of the mountain, I was choking with thirst. I dropped into the shade of a clump of sage and tried to think.

How do you survive in a desert where there isn't any water? I tried to remember everything my father had told me. First, stay near your military equipment so you can use it for shelter. Well, I didn't have any military equipment. Next, keep on all your clothing for protection from the sun. All the clothes I had were my T-shirt, my briefs, jeans, belt, socks, and shoes. And my watch.

There was something else, about a water

distillation gadget. If you've been dropped from an airplane, use your parachute to cover a hole in the ground. Put a basin in the center of the hole to catch water that condenses on the underside of the parachute. If you don't have a parachute, a plastic sheet will work. I didn't have a parachute or a sheet of plastic or a basin, either.

And that was all I could remember.

There was nothing I could do except keep on walking and hope I'd reach the highway soon. As the sun climbed higher over the peak of the mountain, I memorized every feature of that mountain so I'd know where east was. Glancing at the mountain once in a while to check east, I kept my eyes mostly on the north, picking out landmarks ahead of me so I could walk in a straight line. My landmarks were a clump of sagebrush a little taller than the rest, an especially big rock, a rock with an orange stain on it, then a group of big rocks in a circle.

As I got closer to the circle of rocks, I realized that they didn't look natural. Why would those rocks be in a circle when none of the rest of them were? I started to run, and even before I reached them I could see that the inside of the ring of rocks was blackened. Blackened from a fire!

They were a fireplace! Someone had been there! Someone had pushed those big rocks into a circle and built a fire. I dropped to my knees and dug through the sand that had blown inside the circle of rocks. My fingers turned up pieces of charred wood. It had been a fire, all right. Probably made by some campers, but there was no way to tell if it had been just a few days ago or weeks or even months before.

I was so relieved that I threw a handful of ashes and charcoal into the air. If campers had driven out to that spot, I must be heading in the right direction. Maybe more campers would come out and find me. Maybe I wasn't really lost at all!

Something bright and shiny flashed in the sand about a hundred yards ahead of me—the sun was gleaming on metal. As I was running to see where the gleam came from, I squinted to make out what it was, because it was half buried in the sand. Red showed, along with the metal. When I got to it, I yelled because I was so glad.

A six-pack of Coke in a plastic ring holder! I picked it up half expecting the cans to be empty, but they were full! Six full cans! The campers must have forgotten them.

My hands were shaking so much I could

hardly pull up the tab end to punch open one of the cans. When I got it open, a spray of Coke flew up in the air, and I put my mouth over the fizzing hole so I wouldn't lose a single drop. The Coke was warm, but it was still bubbling, and it tasted better than anything I'd ever had in my whole life. I drank it in gulps, even though my throat burned like crazy when I swallowed. Then I opened a second can and drank all of that. I was going to open the third can, but I thought I better save the rest for later.

"I'm going to make it. I'm going to make it," I said out loud, and my voice sounded terrible, like I had laryngitis. But I didn't care. The Coke was rolling around in my stomach and I started to burp, and the burping seemed so funny I had to laugh. I rolled around on the ground laughing, and then I almost cried, but only because I was so happy. "Wait for me, Dad," I said. "I'm coming."

Seven

EVEN the empty Coke cans might be useful for something, so I tucked my T-shirt in my jeans and stuck the cans inside my shirt. I carried the four full cans by the plastic loops.

Whether it was having the Coke inside me or just knowing I had four more twelve-ounce cans, I felt a whole lot better. But it was turning really hot again. "Where's the stupid highway?" I yelled. "Over the next little rise, I bet," I answered myself. But when I could see over the next little rise, the road wasn't there, so I bet myself it would be over the next rise. Only it never was.

Suddenly, I heard a dry, rattling sound right next to me. Rattlesnake! I froze. After a minute I looked on all sides of me, but I couldn't see a snake. I took another step, and I heard the sound again. Then I took another step and found out what was making the noise.

It was a kind of cricket. Sitting still, it looked something like a grasshopper, but when it jumped, wings showed, and it made that rattling noise that scared me so much. I guess I scared it, too, because whenever I moved, it jumped, and when it jumped, it rattled. I had to laugh. Pretty clever of that little cricket to make a sound like a rattlesnake.

I kept looking ahead to spot landmarks so that I could keep walking in a straight line, but now I looked on the ground more carefully, too. If there was anything that other campers had dropped or left behind, I wanted to be sure I found it. And I did find something else, but not from campers. It looked like a piece of rock, but it was black and shiny like glass. It was obsidian. I have lots of it in my rock collection.

Obsidian is volcanic glass, and it can be as sharp as a knife. Indians used it for arrowheads and for scraping hides. They even shaved their heads with it.

You learn lots of things like that when you collect rocks. Rock collecting is a neat hobby for someone who moves around from one part of the country to another, like I did. After we'd settle in a new place, I'd spend a couple of afternoons in the rock shops getting to know the rock and mineral specimens of that area.

Then on weekends, I'd ask my mother—or my dad, if he was home—to drive me out to the countryside so I could rockhound. If they couldn't, I'd go to work on my penny collection. Sorting pennies is a good way to pass the time when you're alone, but rockhounding is more fun.

After I put the obsidian into my pocket, I found another piece, about as big as a baseball cut in half. I put that one in my back pocket.

It was 11:32 by my watch. Almost twenty-four hours since I'd been left in the desert, and I was still alive, thanks to the Coke. The sun was getting high in the sky, and was it ever hot! I thought about hiking to one of the knolls, where maybe I could find some shade under a rock for a couple of hours. But I decided not to waste the time, because I needed to find the highway.

Still, if I didn't get out of the sun for at least a little while, I might get fried like a piece of bacon before I ever found the highway.

Even though I knew there wasn't any shade, I looked around for some. All I saw were sagebrush bushes, but they stood only a foot or two high, and grew too close to the ground to make any shade I could use, now that the sun was so high.

Then I got an idea. If I could break off some

sagebrush branches, maybe I could weave them into a kind of hat to keep the sun off my head.

Sagebrush is tough. It looks like dried-up weed, but the woody branches are wiry. I tugged and pulled, but I couldn't break off any big branches, just small ones. Next I tried jumping, with both feet, on one of the lower branches of a sage. After two minutes of jumping I heard the wood crack, but it took me another couple of minutes to wrestle the branch free from the bush.

By the time the branch came loose, I was sweating. That scared me. There I was, worrying about getting dehydrated by the sun, and at the same time wasting my body's water in sweat. It scared me so much I opened the third can of Coke and drank it. Or maybe I just used the sweating as an excuse, because I wanted to drink that Coke so badly.

Although I needed more branches if I was going to make a hat, I couldn't risk losing sweat to get them. When I sat down to think it over, I landed with a painful bump right on the answer to my problem—the big piece of obsidian in my back pocket.

Indians made cutting tools from obsidian! Neither of my two pieces of obsidian had a sharp edge, the kind that would cut sage. But since Indians chipped their obsidian to make tools, I thought I should be able to chip a cutting edge on one of my pieces.

I put the little piece, the one I'd found first, on a big rock, and tapped it with a smaller rock.

Nothing happened.

I wiggled the tab-end opener on an empty Coke can till it broke off, then I used it like a chisel, holding the metal against the obsidian and tapping it with the small rock.

Still nothing happened.

I got a bigger rock and whacked the metal tab-end against the obsidian. The metal bent, and my fingers got mashed, but the obsidian just sat there, whole.

"How did the Indians do it?" I yelled, getting pretty upset over my throbbing fingers. I put the obsidian onto a big rock and pounded it with another big rock. After a couple of wallops it finally broke—into a hundred tiny, useless chips.

Right about then my logical mind took a vacation. I got so mad that all I wanted to do was smash that dumb obsidian. I pulled the big piece out of my back pocket, put it on a rock, lifted a heavy rock as high as I could, and hurled it down on the obsidian. Somehow, I got lucky. When I looked at the broken pieces, one of them was perfect for cutting. It looked like a knife blade, thin and sharp.

When I tried out the glass-edged blade on a sage branch, it *did* cut, although I had to hack and saw a lot. By the time I'd cut three branches, my head was spinning from heat and hard work.

Next I unlaced one of my Nikes, then laced it again so that one end of the shoestring was real short, just long enough to tie a knot. The other, long end of the shoestring, I cut off with the obsidian. That gave me a piece of shoelace about twelve inches long. I did the same thing with the other shoelace, feeling thankful that Nikes have long shoestrings.

After weaving the sagebrush branches the best I could, I tied them in two places with the cut shoelaces to make my hat. It looked weird, but it held together. Except I couldn't get it to stay on my head.

Well, I couldn't spare any more shoelace, or my shoes would fall off. That left my belt. Snaking the belt through my sagebrush hat, I buckled it under my chin. It worked fine. The hat stayed on, if I didn't bend in any direction.

The sagebrush branches dug into my scalp, but at least my hat kept the sun off my face and neck. Still, I wondered whether it had been worth the trouble. I'd wasted a lot of time when I could have been looking for the highway, and the work had really tired me out.

I was so tired . . . from heat and thirst and walking and struggling with the sagebrush. But it was strange: I'd stopped being hungry. If I'd come across a cheeseburger and French fries lying on the sand (some dreamer!), I probably wouldn't have bothered to pick them up. Because even if I'd been hungry, which I wasn't, it would have hurt too much to swallow anything solid.

But thirst! That was something else. I never for a single minute stopped being thirsty. Each time, right after I'd finished a can of Coke, I'd still wanted more to drink. Each time, I'd had to talk myself out of punching open the next can.

And as if I weren't miserable enough from heat and thirst and from the sagebrush hat digging into my head, I started to feel miserable from worry, because I knew I should have spotted the highway by that time. I'd been walking steadily, slogging through sand, from the time I'd finished making my hat. Counting all the walking from the day before, I figured I must have covered a good ten miles. With the sun straight up overhead, it was getting hard to figure out exactly where north was. I might have gotten turned around somehow, or maybe the highway didn't lie directly north.

That's what worried me.

Each step got harder to take. Finally I had to stop and rest. Where I stopped, two sagebrush bushes a little taller than the rest were growing about eighteen inches apart. I took off my sagebrush hat and balanced it between the top edges of the two bushes. It stayed put, and it made shade! Not much, but enough for me to crawl between the bushes and lie on my back. My face was in the shade, and when I crossed my arms over my chest, my arms were pretty much shaded, too.

Before my eyes drooped shut, I noticed something dirty white sticking on a branch of one of the bushes, a clump of woolly fuzz like from a blanket. People must camp all over this desert, I thought. That was the last thought I had before I fell into a deep sleep.

Pain in my arms woke me up. The sagebrush hat had fallen to the ground, leaving me stretched out in full sunlight. My arms were really broiled. They were brick red and too sore to touch. But what made my stomach lurch was the things I saw sticking to my arms. Three ticks.

I knew they were ticks because we had a dog once, and he used to go running through the woods and come home with ticks in his ears. Ticks are horrible bugs. They fasten onto your skin and suck your blood until their bodies swell up, and even after they're full they don't drop off for a long, long time. You can't pull them off, because if you try to, their bodies break off and the heads stay stuck in your skin.

The best way to get rid of a tick is to burn it. Dad used to light wooden matches, then blow them out and stick the hot tips against the swollen tick bodies on our dog. That made the bugs' mouths let loose, and they fell off.

I sat up, feeling my skin crawl as I fought the impulse to tear off the ticks, wondering how I could burn them off since I didn't have any matches. Sitting up so fast made my head spin. Maybe I'd better drink another Coke, I thought, so I can figure this out with a clearer head. So I did.

Fire. How can you make fire? By rubbing two sticks together—that would take forever— or by holding a magnifying glass under the sun's rays. I had plenty of sun—too much— but I didn't have a magnifying glass.

I did have a lens, though! My military watch had a thick, curved lens. If I took the watch apart, the lens might work like a magnifying glass. I could hold it over the ticks and burn them off.

With the tab-end from the Coke can, I pried

off the back of the watch, putting the insides into my pocket. When I held the lens over the fat, ugly tick on my left arm, the sun's rays shining through it *did* come to a point. And it was hot enough, because I burned my arm with it before I zeroed in on the tick. It worked! The first tick fell off. Yay!

I got the second one off, too. But when I held the lens over the third tick, the one on my right arm, I couldn't make any point of light. Puzzled, I looked at the sky and found that the sun had gone behind clouds. In fact, the whole sky was darkening.

I slid the sharp point of my obsidian knife under the last tick and cut a little hole in my arm, hoping I got the whole tick head out, knowing I probably didn't. By that time I didn't care so much because I was excited about the clouds in the sky. It looked like it was going to rain. If there was anything I needed, it was rain! Rain would cool my burning skin, and give me something to drink. Of course, I still had two cans of Coke, but that wasn't much, and I was awful thirsty, as usual.

Dad had told me that a person needs a gallon of water a day to stay alive in the desert, because the sun and wind dry out your body so much faster than normal. My whole supply for the day was six cans times twelve ounces of Coke. I didn't know how many ounces were in a gallon, but it had to be a whole lot more than I'd found. If it rained and I could catch some rain water, maybe I could make up some of the difference.

Sitting on the sand, sucking the blood from the cut in my arm, I watched the sky as more and more clouds rolled in. A jagged streak of lightning shot from one cloud to another, followed by a low boom of thunder. Dirty gray clouds piled up one on top of the other in the sky right over my head, and more streaks of lightning slashed through the sky. The bottom edges of the gray clouds hung down like torn curtains.

I waited for the rain to drop on me, but instead, a flash of lightning hit the ground really close by, and the thunder nearly split my eardrums. More lightning exploded all around me, with blinding, crackling flashes of light, and thunder that felt like it would blow my head off. I was so scared I threw myself facedown on the ground and covered my head with my arms, because I was sure I was going to get hit. After what seemed like forever, but was probably only a couple of minutes, the lightning moved farther away, and I got brave enough to look at the sky again.

It was raining in the sky, all right, but no

drops fell on me. Wind was blowing, a warm, gritty wind that stung my burning skin. The clouds above me were rolling around, turning inside out. Rain was falling, but why wasn't any of it falling on me?

The raindrops never reached the ground. Gray streaks of rain curved downward from the bottoms of the clouds, but the drops evaporated in midair, somewhere between the sky and the desert floor. I couldn't believe it! Whoever heard of rain that didn't make it all the way to the ground? My throat choked up and I wanted to bawl, because the rain was right up above me but it wouldn't come down where I needed it.

It was raining on the tops of the mountains, though, I could see that. And if it was raining on the tops, the water might run down to the lower parts of the mountain. I fought back the scare from the thunder and lightning, and the feeling so sorry for myself about the rain, because I had to make a decision.

Should I take time to go to the nearest mountain, hoping to find rainwater, or should I keep pushing for the highway and try to get by on the two cans of Coke I had left?

I started to look at my watch, but remembered it was in pieces inside my pocket. I took out the watch part, which was still in the back of the case, and looked at it: 14:40—20 to 3. It had to be later than that! It had been 14:32 when I took the watch apart. I put my hand into my jeans pocket and felt about a teaspoon of sand. Sand must have worked into the watch gears when I put it in my pocket. I shook the watch, then blew on it and held it to my ear to hear if the battery was still running. It wasn't. My watch, my beautiful watch . . . It was ruined.

Everything was going wrong for me! Why couldn't anything go right? Why couldn't I find the dumb highway? Why did I have to get into this mess in the first place? I got so frustrated that I hauled back my arm and threw the watchworks as far as I could into the desert. I threw away the case and strap, with the lens, too, and then I started to cry in great big sobs that tore out of my chest. Sprawled flat, I pounded the desert because I felt too young and scared to handle all the bad things that were happening to me.

I couldn't control my crying, even though I knew that tears were wasting water my body couldn't spare. I cried until I got so worn out that I didn't have the strength for another sob, and then I lay there for a long time, feeling wrung out, but a little better. After a while I sat up. I still had to decide about going up the mountain.

One part of me was saying, "Look, the highway's got to be near. You can make it on two cans of Coke. Forget about the rainwater in the mountains."

But another part of me said, "Face up to it. You're really lost. If there's any water on the mountain, you'd better get it fast before it dries up. Otherwise, you won't stay alive long enough to reach your dad. Remember, it's DD Day Minus Three."

I groaned, because I knew the second voice was right.

Eight

SO I had to climb the mountain.
I debated whether to take the two full
Coke cans with me. It would be hard carrying
them while I was dragging myself up the
mountain. If I left the cans next to the sagebrush bushes, I could spread my T-shirt on
top of the bushes as a marker, so I could find
my way back to them.

But I couldn't bring myself to leave the
Coke behind. Just the feel of those two cans in
my hands, the weight of their fullness, gave me
some bit of hope that I might make it, I might
get back to my father before it was too late.
The bright red of the metal was so real, so
man-made, compared to the dull color of the
emptiness around me. If I'd been sinking in
the ocean, I would have felt about a life jacket
the way I felt about that Coke. Still, it would
be tough to hold those cans while I was

climbing.

Since the sky was still gray and overcast, I didn't need to wear my sagebrush hat. Pulling my belt out of it, I slid the belt through the loops of my jeans, then buckled it loosely. That gave me room to shove the two full Coke cans inside the belt. The four empties I wanted to take with me, too, to fill with water if I found any. I put them inside my shirt. The plastic loops that had held the cans looked like they might be useful for something, but I couldn't figure out what, so I threw them away.

The nearest elevation was another of the low, craggy-topped knolls like the one I'd climbed the day before. Loaded down with Coke cans, carrying my sagebrush hat because I didn't want to leave it behind, I made pretty slow progress toward the knoll. More than once I stumbled and fell on my hands and knees. Then the Coke cans would tumble out of my belt, and I'd have to repack my cargo before I could start again.

By the time I reached the bottom of the knoll, I was wondering if I'd been crazy to come. The bottom was bone-dry. But since I'd gone so far, I figured I might as well climb up partway. If rain had reached the top of the knoll, the rainwater would have to run down, and it might collect in hollows in the rock.

Since I needed both hands and feet for climbing, I left my sagebrush hat at the bottom of the knoll, where I could pick it up on my way back. The first part of the climb wasn't hard, but when I got to the steep part, I had to pull myself over boulders. A pointed rock caught my T-shirt and yanked it right out of my jeans. Before I could catch it, one of the empty Coke cans fell out and went clattering down the side of the knoll until it disappeared. I stuck my shirt back into my jeans and pulled my belt a notch tighter, so I wouldn't lose the other three empties.

Pretty soon I saw the first sign of raindrops—they'd left spatter marks in the red dust. I climbed higher, checking every gouge in the rocks, till I came to a big flat boulder with a hollow in the top. Half an inch of water stood in the hollow.

Crouching over the puddle, I sucked it up. There wasn't much. I was afraid to take time to rest because the sun might start to shine again, and I wanted to find more water, if there was any, before it all dried up.

So I kept climbing and found another small puddle. The water was muddy, but it was deep enough for me to half fill one of my empty cans and drink. Then I lapped the rest like a dog. By that time I was so tired I just had to stop and rest.

Sitting on a big boulder with my feet dangling over the edge, I closed my eyes so I wouldn't have to look at that miserable, deadly, sage-filled desert far below. When I heard a rattling sound, I glanced down expecting to see a cricket. But this time it wasn't a cricket. It was a rattlesnake.

Coiled in the dirt about eighteen inches below my feet, the snake had his flat head raised high and was sticking out his black tongue in quick little darts. I was scared to move. I remembered that Dad had said, "If you come across a snake, hold still and give him a chance to get away. He's more afraid of you than you are of him."

So I sat perfectly still—more from fright than good sense—and waited for him to go away. Only, he must not have known that he was supposed to be afraid of me. He just stared at me, his shiny eyes never blinking, his body slowly curving back and forth. I raised my feet a little, but his head shot up and his rattles buzzed, so I held myself like a statue. After what seemed an awful long time, the snake slowly turned away and slithered into a pile of rocks.

I let out my breath. My heart was pounding so hard I could feel it hit my ribs.

I wanted to leap away and run down from that knoll as fast as possible, but I waited until the snake had plenty of time to get wherever he was going. After that I came close to breaking my neck getting down, sliding on the seat of my pants until I reached the valley floor.

But I must have gone down a different way than I went up, because I couldn't see my sagebrush hat! I looked as far as I could see, in every direction, but one bunch of sagebrush looks pretty much like another, and sage was all over the place. I just couldn't find my hat. All that work, all for nothing! I felt bad, but I'd had so many disasters already that I was too numb to react much.

The storm hadn't cooled things at all. Although the sky was still cloudy, the heat was as bad as ever. The skin on my arms started to rise up in big, puffy blisters, and I knew my face and neck must be doing the same. My skin looked so repulsive that I was ready to drop on the sand and just quit trying, give up looking for the road, die all at once and get it over with, instead of having parts of me die one at a time, starting with my skin.

I think I really would have given up then, if I hadn't made my second important discovery of the day.

When you're looking at miles and miles of

nothing but sand and sagebrush, anything unusual sort of reaches out and taps you on the eyeballs. From a distance, I couldn't figure out what was waving out there, but when I got close enough, I saw that it was a dusty sheet of plastic caught on the branches of a sage. Probably it was used as a ground cloth by a camping party. The wind had blown it until it got stuck on the sage.

I stood there and stared at it for a full five minutes before my mind took in the possibilities. That dusty sheet of plastic was just what I needed to make a water distillation unit, and I even had the empty cans to catch the water in.

I was so excited by my discovery that I drank my last two cans of Coke to celebrate. I didn't have to worry any more about water, my crazy, mixed-up brain told me, because I knew how to get water by using the plastic sheet. That just shows how fried my brain was getting.

Sure, I could make a water distillation unit, but I couldn't carry the hole in the ground with me! It took hours for one of those things to work. If I built a water still, I'd have to wait for the cans to fill up, probably till the next day. And if I waited, I couldn't walk toward the highway. But I didn't catch on to that fact until after my last two cans of Coke were inside me.

Well, there was nothing to do except pack up the plastic sheet and the cans and keep on walking; I'd have the stuff with me if I needed to spend another night in the desert. So I walked, and then I had to stop because muscle cramps in my legs were killing me. Then I walked some more, and I got stomach cramps so painful they doubled me over. It felt like I'd been punched in the gut.

I've been beat up a couple times—I know what it feels like to be slugged in the stomach. It feels awful. Only a few weeks before school let out, a big, tough seventh grader named Garth started slapping me around. "I've had my eye on you ever since you came to this school," Garth told me while he was punching me out. "I just want you to know we don't like outsiders in this town. Especially a military brat. Because war is immoral!" he yelled, hammering my gut.

After he'd finished with me and I was lying on the playground, trying to get my breath back, two guys from my sixth-grade class came to help me up. Their names were Paul and Stuart.

Stuart wiped the blood off my elbows with wet paper towels, while Paul picked up my books and homework papers. "Don't feel bad about Garth," Paul said. "He's a weird creep and he gets his jollies out of beating up on smaller kids."

"Yeah," Stuart said. "Just stay out of his way."

If it hadn't been so close to the end of the school year, I might have got to know Paul and Stuart better. They were nice guys. They said hi when they saw me, in school or out. I'm going back to that California school in September, so maybe it could work out that we'll be friends.

I curled on the sand to rest till the cramps eased up. Either I slept or I passed out, because when I came to, the light seemed to be fading.

I'd had good luck in one way, at least. After the thunderstorm, the sky had stayed overcast for the rest of the day. That was a good thing, because my eyelids were swollen from sunburn and my eyes had become sore from glare. The cloudiness, and the beginning of evening, made it cooler, too, so I could walk farther. At least I thought I could, but my body didn't believe me. It just wouldn't keep moving.

My strength was about gone. Since it looked like I was going to spend the night where I was, I decided to make the water distillation unit. Stomping one of the cans, I flattened it so I could use it to dig the hole for the water still.

"Wait a minute," I said. (I was talking to myself a lot by that time.) "You have four cans left, so make four stills."

The plastic sheet was about five feet square. Very carefully, using the sharp obsidian to cut it, I divided it into four equal pieces. To make the four holes, I dug with the flattened can and scooped out the sand with one of my shoes. I hoped the holes were deep enough.

The hardest job was cutting the tops off the four empty Coke cans. It was a good thing the cans were made of soft aluminum. My cutting tool was the piece of obsidian. Hitting it with a rock, I went around the top edges of the cans like a can opener. When I finished, my hands were bleeding.

In the center of each of the four holes in the ground I put a Coke can. Then, with my T-shirt, I wiped as much dust off the plastic as I could. I covered each of the holes with a piece of plastic, weighing them down around the edges with rocks and sand, because the wind had started up again, although not as bad as the night before. I put a small rock in the center of each sheet of plastic to make it dip in the middle, right above the can. If things worked the way they were supposed to, moisture from the ground would rise to the underside of the plastic, condense, roll down the sides and drip into the cans. If they worked the way they were supposed to.

By the time I finished it was dark. The sky had cleared and was filling with stars again, but I didn't even want to look at them. Since my watch was gone, I didn't know for sure what time it was, but I figured I'd been in the desert for at least thirty-two hours. Dad had said a person could survive for twenty-four hours. That meant my time had already run out, but I was too tired to worry about it.

Sprawled on the sand, I fell into a deep sleep that lasted until I woke up shaking with cold. A faint brightening showed in the sky to the east.

DD Day Minus Two was beginning.

Nine

I lay on the ground in the early-morning darkness, wondering if there would be any water in the cans, but I was too scared to go and look. Because if there wasn't any, I was finished. I had nothing else to drink.

After the sky turned light enough for me to see what I was doing, I rolled over and tried to get up. My body wouldn't cooperate. My arms and legs felt like they belonged to four different people, and I couldn't get them all to work together.

When I did manage to stand, dizziness almost knocked me down again. My head pounded, every bone in my body ached, and I felt like I needed to throw up, if I'd had anything inside me to throw up. Instead of walking to the water stills, I staggered.

With shaking hands, I pulled back the sheet of plastic covering the first hole. I lifted the can. There was water in it, but not much. Less than an inch. I guess I hadn't dug the holes deep enough. I sipped it, holding the water in my mouth for a long time before my swollen throat would swallow. It tasted sandy, but who cared?

After I swallowed what was in the next three cans, I licked the undersides of the plastic sheets, getting more grit than moisture. And that was that. No more water.

Then I noticed my arms. Big, ugly-looking blisters puckered my skin from my shoulders to my knuckles. They looked so horrible, they made my stomach turn even sicker.

For a long time I sat on the sand trying to decide whether to take the empty cans and the plastic sheets with me. My head felt like it was full of Brillo pads—I couldn't think straight. Finally I put the empty cans on the plastic sheets and pulled the corners together, to make a sack that I could carry.

If it took me a long time to think, it took even longer to do things. I seemed to be moving in slow motion. By the time I was ready to start out, the sun was up and getting hot.

I'd walk a couple of steps, then fall. After three or four falls, it didn't make sense to get up again, so I left the water distillation stuff behind, and just crawled. Pictures of all those

Saturday-morning cartoons came to m
the ones where Bugs Bunny and other
ters crawl on the desert, croaking, "
Water!" I laughed inside my head, but no
sound came out through my cracked lips.

I don't know how many times I passed out,
or how long I stayed out. Once I woke up lying
on my back, and fought to open my eyes. My
eyelids were so puffy that I was looking
through narrow slits. The sun didn't look like a
sun was supposed to. It was flat, a disk
without any color. As I watched, the sun got
bigger and turned bloody red, with purple and
orange circles around it.

That was when my brain went crazy.

Bright streaks of flame shot over my head,
bursting like fireworks. They were mortars
exploding—I could hear enemy shellfire. I was
in a desert in the Middle East, caught in
crossfire, and I couldn't find a bunker to hide
in.

Ahead of me, forty feet away on the sand,
my father was stretched out. He'd been hit!
His face was all bloody, and blood seeped
through his combat shirt.

"Medics! Medics!" I screamed, but nobody
came. I'd have to rescue my dad, or he'd die!
Shells exploded all around me, and bullets
zinged so close above my head that I stayed

flat and wiggled forward like a snake. Maybe I'd been hit, too. I didn't know, but I had to keep going.

When I reached my dad, his eyes were closed, and his skin was deathly white under that red blood. I got my left arm beneath his shoulder to drag him along with me, pulling myself with my right elbow. I was surprised, because my dad didn't weigh anything, even though he's a big man six feet tall. We had so far to go—miles and miles—and it was taking us weeks to get there. Red days and purple nights passed. Still I kept dragging my dad.

We'd got out of the line of shellfire, but machine-gun fire took over—*ma-a-a-a-a, ma-a-a-a-a,* louder and louder the farther I crawled. When I raised my head, I saw enemy soldiers in the distance, dressed in dirty gray uniforms. The machine-gun fire got heavier, *ma-a-a-a, ma-a-a-a, ma-a-a-a.*

Then I saw why they were shooting at us. They were defending a water hole, the only water in the desert. Some of the enemy soldiers were in the water hole up to their knees; others stood around the edges. Dad and I had to take that water hole—that was our military objective.

I looked up, and Dad was towering over me, standing upright with his legs spread apart. He was alive, healthy, and about ten feet tall. "Come on, Kevin," he shouted. "You can do it. Just a little farther."

And I did it! I reached the water and fell into it facedown. It tasted awful, warm and salty and yucky, but it was water, real water! I guess the shock of the water started to clear my head, because when I jerked up for air, the enemy was gone and I was surrounded by a bunch of sheep. Big sheep that were *ma-a-a, ma-a-a-a*-ing like mad, bumping into one another trying to get away from me.

Someone grabbed me by the shoulders and I felt myself half lifted and half dragged out of the water, and I fought and screamed and yelled, "Let me go, Dad! Let me drink!"

A voice answered, "No, NO! This water's no good, make you sick. This water's for sheep only—see, it's piped from underground, all salty. Come with me, don't fight. I'll give you good water."

And then I was lying on the dry ground while an old man knelt over me, holding a canteen to my lips. "A little at a time, that's a good fella," he said. "Take it easy."

My head felt like I was fighting my way out of a terrible nightmare, trying to come awake. "Take it easy, take it easy," the man kept saying. "Where did you come from?"

My eyes started to focus, and I saw that the old man's face was twisted like he was looking at something horrible—me! His thick eyebrows shot up, and he asked, "Are you the boy Kevin Hoffman, the one missing from Spriggs?"

I nodded, not even wondering how he knew.

"Oi, oi, yami!" he said. He lifted me in his arms and carried me somewhere—I didn't care where, I wasn't thinking, just feeling relieved. Someone had found me, now someone else would have to take over worrying about whether I stayed alive. It was all right for me to give up, to stop trying.

In a daze, I saw that he was carrying me to a little trailer that looked like a covered wagon made of sheet metal, with a crooked chimney sticking out of the roof. He climbed through a door and laid me on a bunk.

"What day is it?" I whispered.

"Tuesday, Wednesday, what's the difference?" he answered. "I don't know."

I tried again. "What date?"

The old man took off his cowboy hat and scratched his head, peering at a calendar tacked on the wall. "I guess June nineteenth."

I sighed. It was still DD Day Minus Two. I'd made it. I slept.

When I woke up, the old man was holding a

tin cup full of broth. "Drink this," he said, touching a spoon against my lips. Something damp was on my forehead. I reached to touch it. It was a wet towel. "Try to swallow this stuff," he said. "It will help you. You're gonna be okay." But the worried look on his face made me wonder if he was telling the truth.

After a few swallows I asked, "Who are you?"

"Me? Santiago Aquirre, sheepherder. I'm a Basque from the Pyrenees Mountains in Spain, but I herd sheep in this country for fifty years, since I was a boy like you."

"How did you know who I was?"

"From the radio." He pointed to a battery portable on the table. "Everyone is looking for you. Police, airplanes, everyone. Everyone's worried that you been killed by escaped crooks. How did you get in Deabru?"

"What?" I didn't understand.

"Deabru, the Devil. I call this desert Deabru because it is hot like Hell and hard to get out of. How did you get here?"

"Jumped out of the truck. They left me here. Can I call my mother and father?"

Santiago smiled. "You think I got a telephone out here in Deabru? We got to drive to the Peterson ranch, about a hour and a half from here."

"What time is it?" I asked.

"I never saw such a boy for worrying about time," Santiago said. "Time, date, I don't pay so much attention." He opened the door and stuck his head out to look at the sky. "Sun says about one o'clock."

He came back and looked down at me, his hands on his hips. "You think you're strong enough for a truck ride?"

"Yeah," I told him. I didn't really feel strong enough—I felt so weak and sick I didn't even want to move a finger, but more than anything else I wanted my parents.

"Okay. First I'll go tell my *txakurrak*—'scuse me, I said that in Basque—tell my sheep dogs to take care of the herd till I get back. Then I'll come get you and put you in the truck. Don't try to stand up or nothing."

While Santiago was outside, I looked around the trailer. It was like a little house, with a table and chair, stacks of cans on a shelf, and big bottles of water. Next to the calendar, a cross hung on the wall, and above that was a long rifle.

When the sheepherder came back and carried me to his pickup truck, he said, "You better not sit up. Lay on the seat sideways, feet on the floor. I'm gonna drive fast, so we'll bounce a lot, but we got to get you some doctor help pretty quick."

The bouncing was bad, all right. Weak as I was, I couldn't sleep from all that bucking around. Seeing that I was awake, Santiago started to talk about himself. "You rest, I'll talk," he said.

He'd left the Pyrenees Mountains because his family was so poor. When he got to Utah, he was sent out in the desert with one dog and a thousand sheep.

"That first summer I nearly went crazy with loneliness," he told me, "and winter was worse. I was sixteen. I thought only about home, and I cried every day. But after a couple of years, it wasn't so bad. Basques are the best sheepherders in the world because they can stand loneliness."

Even though my head felt as though a load of cinder blocks was sitting on it, something jabbed at my mind, a question I had to ask Santiago. "I saw little balls of manure from jackrabbits all over the desert," I managed to say. "Where do the rabbits drink?"

"Nah, that wasn't from jackrabbits," Santiago said. "You saw droppings from my sheep. Anyway, jackrabbits don't need to drink. They get water out of what they eat— grass and shrubs. The only water in all of Deabru is my sheep pond."

For a while after that Santiago was quiet. Then, when the truck tires suddenly made a different sound, he said, "We're on highway now."

"Jeez!" I croaked. "I've been looking for the highway for three days."

"But you came towards my sheep camp," Santiago said. "You been headed the wrong direction."

Ten

STILL holding me in his arms, Santiago knocked on the door of a ranch house. The door was opened by a woman, who gasped when she saw me.

"This is the boy Kevin Hoffman, the one missing from Spriggs, Señora Peterson," Santiago told her. "I found him about noon at my sheep camp. He's in bad shape."

"Bring him inside, Santiago," she said, throwing open the door. "Good heavens! I'll call my husband. Einar, Einar!" she shouted, sounding really flustered.

The man must have been close enough to hear what Santiago had said, because he was beside us right away. "Put him over there on the sofa. Holy blazes! He looks . . . " He didn't finish saying what I looked like.

"Call my father, please," I whispered. "He's in Spriggs."

"What's the number, honey?" Mrs. Peterson asked, bending over me. But I didn't know Gram's number.

"Never mind, I'll call the state police," she said. "They'll reach your folks, and they'll send help."

When Mrs. Peterson picked up the phone, she looked annoyed. "Elvira, get off the line," she said.

"We have a party line," Mr. Peterson explained.

"Please, Elvira," she was saying, "this is an emergency. The missing boy from Spriggs is here in our living room. No, I don't know what happened to him. No, Elvira, don't come over here . . . ."

"Give me that phone," Mr. Peterson yelled, pulling the receiver out of his wife's hand. "Elvira, get off the line this minute!" he roared, then slammed down the receiver, hard. "That woman has a mouth like an electric mixer!"

He lifted the phone again and punched in the numbers. "State police? This is Einar Peterson, from the Lazy Seven Ranch, thirty-five miles northwest of Delta. We have the missing boy from Spriggs here. Yes, he's alive, but just barely. He was out in the desert, for quite a while from the looks of him. He's going to need medical attention as soon as possible. And call his folks in Spriggs, will you? Yeah . . . that's right . . . okay. Our number's 157-3812."

Santiago Aquirre knelt beside me. "Kevin, I got to go now. Can't leave the dogs alone with the sheep too long, or they'll ask for a raise in pay."

"Couldn't you wait till my folks get here?" I asked him, holding his hand. I didn't want Santiago to go. I felt as though I'd known him forever, like he was a close relative. "They'll want to thank you for saving my life."

"Nah, I didn't save your life. I just found you. You saved your own life. You're a brave fella, a *gizon sua*."

Smiling at me, Santiago gently loosened my fingers. "You come see me sometime, Kevin. When you're all better."

The door had just closed behind him when the telephone rang.

"That was a doctor," Mr. Peterson said after he hung up. "A woman doctor. She told me that we mustn't give Kevin anything to eat or drink, or he'll get bad stomach cramps. Just cover him with a blanket, she said, and let him rest till the medics get here."

"Oh, dear. I was just about to give him some lemonade." Mrs. Peterson set a pitcher and a glass on an end table next to the sofa, saying,

"I'll go get a blanket."

The pitcher was chrome—when I glanced at it, I saw my face reflected. Then I knew why everyone acted shocked when they first saw me.

My hair wasn't dark any more. It was so full of dust that it had turned sand colored, and it was matted like a worn-out scrub brush. My face looked beet red under the dirt; so swollen that my eyes were thin slits. The skin on my cheeks was puffy, but at the same time wrinkled and withered. My lips were cracked, caked with dried blood. I had to close my eyes because I couldn't stand to look at myself.

I guess Mrs. Peterson thought I was asleep, because she tiptoed to cover me with the blanket. It felt so warm and comfortable—maybe I did fall asleep, because the next thing I knew, Mrs. Peterson was touching my shoulder, saying, "A police car is coming down our road." She pulled the curtain to get a better look. "Four people are in it—two troopers . . . and your parents, it looks like."

And then my mother was running toward me with her arms open wide, and this time I sure intended to let her hug me. But my dad shouted from right behind her, "Don't hug him, Diane! He's so badly sunburned that any pressure could damage his skin."

They dropped to their knees next to me. Mom kissed her fingertips, and almost, but not quite, touched the kiss to my sore lips.

I don't remember all the things we said, but the words meant that we were happy to see each other. Everyone was crying, even Mr. Peterson, I think.

"Nellis Air Force Base is sending a helicopter," Dad told me. "I talked to the base commander after we heard from the police. He said to bring you to the base hospital there because they have an excellent burn unit."

All this time the state troopers had been standing just inside the door, as though they didn't want to disturb our family reunion. I heard one tell the other that they'd better go outside and flag the area for the helicopter, so the pilot would know where to set down.

"How's Barney?" I asked my parents.

"He has a headache and a bandage around his head, but he'll be fine," Mom answered. "Barney says the gasoline can got a bigger dent in it than his skull did."

"There's another car pulling up outside," Mrs. Peterson announced. "They're getting out . . . It looks like a bunch of news people. They have cameras. How did they ever find out . . . ? Oh . . . ! That Elvira!"

"Don't let them in!" Mr. Peterson hollered.

We could hear him talking in a loud voice to some people outside the door, but more important, we heard helicopter blades chugging above the ranch house.

Then, a lot of confusion. Medical corpsmen put me on a stretcher and carried me outside. Flashbulbs went off, and a TV camera whirred right next to my face. A second chopper landed—Mom and Dad were to ride in that one. I barely had time to say thanks to the Petersons before I was strapped to a basket on the floor of the chopper, and we lifted off.

Eleven

THE hospital people had everything waiting. I was hardly inside the emergency room before the doctors and nurses started another IV. The medics had already begun one when I was in the helicopter. It dripped saltwater solution into my body through a needle in my leg.

The worst part was when they cleaned my burned skin. They tried to be gentle, but the whole thing was really painful, and it lasted a long time. Then they put burn medicine on me and wrapped my arms with bandages.

Night had come by the time the orderlies wheeled me into my hospital room. Mom turned on the TV, and there I was, on the ten o'clock news. I felt myself blushing underneath my sunburn. "Oh, yuck! How repulsive," I muttered. It was embarrassing that millions of TV viewers would see me looking so ugly.

After he'd talked about me, the announcer said, "The escaped convicts who left Kevin Hoffman in the desert were apprehended early today at the Goshute Indian Reservation on the Utah-Nevada border. From a report released by the Utah State Department of Prisons, Channel Twelve has learned that the two criminals had been hiding on the reservation since shortly after their stolen truck ran out of gas, close to the reservation border. When one of the convicts attempted to buy groceries at the trading post this morning, tribal police arrested the man, who then led them to the second convict."

Dad let out a deep breath. "So they caught those rotten—"

"What will happen to them?" I asked.

"I hope the authorities throw the book at them," Dad snapped, sounding really angry. "I imagine they'll be charged with robbery, assault, kidnapping, and attempted murder."

"Attempted murder!" I squeaked.

"Absolutely. Those men knew that abandoning you in the desert was like killing you in cold blood. What they couldn't know was that you"—Dad's voice kind of choked up—"are a very extraordinary boy."

"Major Hoffman, Mrs. Hoffman." A nurse had come into my room. "You'd better let

Kevin get some sleep. I suspect you two could use some sleep yourselves."

"We'll be back first thing in the morning," Mom told me.

* * * * *

DD Day Minus One.

Mom and Dad stayed with me all the time, even though I slept through most of the day. Later in the afternoon, Dr. Allen came in to take blood samples. Dr. Allen (or Captain Allen, I could never figure out which to call her) told us, "When Kevin became dehydrated, his body salts were depleted. We'll do a blood analysis every day, until his salt balance gets back to normal. After that, we can take out the IV."

"How long will that be?" I asked her.

"Probably a week. Then you'll be able to get out of bed, and you can start eating regular meals. They make pretty good tacos here at the base hospital. That'll give you something to look forward to."

Even though I've always been quiet around strangers, in the hospital I couldn't help talking to people. Dr. Allen, and the nurses, and even the orderlies who cleaned my room kept asking me questions about what happened, if I was awake when they came in. They seemed really interested in what I told them. And, of course, Mom and Dad had to hear everything.

I felt ashamed to admit to my dad what I'd done with my watch, but he just said, "Don't worry about it, son. I probably would have done the same thing."

I made myself stay awake during the evening, because the next day Dad would be flying out. He couldn't tell me the exact time he was leaving—it was top secret. Funny, we talked mostly about my days in the desert. We said very little about his leaving. I didn't want to upset him with my own fears, and I guess he understood.

The usual hospital sleeping pill knocked me out, so I slept really hard. During the night, I sensed that my father was beside me, but I couldn't manage to come awake. In the morning, though, I was certain he'd been there.

The package was lying on the hospital blanket, right next to my hand. When I opened it, I found another military watch, exactly like the one I'd left in the desert. There was no note, but there didn't need to be. I knew it was from Dad, and I knew what he was telling me. That he loved me, and he was proud of me. I couldn't wear the watch because of the bandages, but I kept it beside me, to touch every few minutes.

When Mom came in, her faced showed that she'd been crying. I wanted to comfort her, because I wasn't scared about Dad any more. Maybe it was the feel of the watch beneath my fingertips. It was sort of an omen, a sign that we'd have plenty of time left to us, after he came back. Before I could explain those feelings to my mom, she held out a pile of mail.

"Look what came for you, Kevin. More than three dozen cards and letters from all over the country. People must have learned about you from the television newscasts."

I was really surprised. I sorted through the pile, looking at the return addresses. All that mail from people I didn't even know! Then I noticed a familiar California postmark.

"Hey, look!" I said. "Here's a letter from Paul. And here's another one, from Stuart. They must have written right away, right after the early news."

I'd started to tear open the envelopes from Stuart and Paul, but I stopped, because I could tell that Mom had something she wanted to say to me. Sitting on the edge of my bed, she reached as though she wanted to touch my hand, but pulled back.

"It's okay," I told her. "You can hold the

palm of my hand, if you want to. That part isn't sore."

She covered my hand with hers, and said, "It's just . . . you've been through so much, Kevin. First, that terrible ordeal in the desert, and then having Dad leave so soon after you were rescued. I want you to know that I'm certain Dad's going to return safely. When he does, your life will be the way it used to."

"You know what, Mom? I've been feeling the same way, and if both of us feel it, it's got to be right. Only there's one correction," I said, sliding my arm around her. "My life isn't going to be the way it was. It's going to be even better."

After I gave her a long, careful hug, I began to read the letters from my friends.

About the Author

GLORIA SKURZYNSKI has the ability to research and explain medicine, geography, and scientific phenomena. This is equalled by her flair for characterization and suspense.

Her information is checked by experts in the United States natural resource agencies.

Gloria Skurzynski lives in Salt Lake City, Utah.